DEATH BY DIDGERIDOO

JAMIE QUINN COZY MYSTERIES BOOK 1

BARBARA VENKATARAMAN

Copyright (C) 2021 Barbara Venkataraman

Layout design and Copyright (C) 2021 by Next Chapter

Published 2021 by Next Chapter

Cover art by CoverMint

Large Print Edition

This book is a work of fiction. Names, characters, places, and incidents are the product of the author's imagination or are used fictitiously. Any resemblance to actual events, locales, or persons, living or dead, is purely coincidental.

All rights reserved. No part of this book may be reproduced or transmitted in any form or by any means, electronic or mechanical, including photocopying, recording, or by any information storage and retrieval system, without the author's permission.

For all of their support, advice and enthusiasm, I want to thank all of my "reader girls:" Janet, Jodi, Joette, Kahlia, Linda, Mai, Michele, Myra and Nanette.

CHAPTER 1

I DON'T KNOW WHY I FEEL GUILTY, IT'S NOT LIKE I killed the guy. I didn't even know him, but I heard he was a real bastard. Let me put it this way, when word got out that Spike was dead, that he'd been murdered with one of his own musical instruments, celebrations broke out all over town. Some people toasted his demise with expensive champagne, while others clinked bottles of cold beer; it just depended on the neighborhood. And while many stories were told that night--none of them complimentary, I assure you--there was a common theme: Spike was a liar and a cheat, a poor excuse for a man who'd steal from his own mother, if he knew where she was, or sleep with a friend's wife, if he had a friend--which he did not. Spike's only companion was his dog, Beast, a German shepherd that went everywhere he did, and wasn't very friendly either.

You're probably wondering how Spike had such a successful music store when he was *such* a major jerk. The answer is simple--he was a rock star. Literally. His drum solos were legendary. After *The Screaming Zombies'* first album, **Deathlock,** went platinum in 1999 and Spike won drummer of the year, there seemed to be no stopping this garage band of high school dropouts. But Spike found a way. With his huge ego and flair for paranoia, he managed to piss off everyone in no time, including the band's manager, agent, publicist, producer, all the way up to the head of the record label. The roadies especially despised him. They would set his drums up the wrong way or turn his speakers off whenever they could get away with it. And let's not forget the rest of *The Screaming Zombies*, Snake, Slasher and Slime, a/k/a Daryl, Marcus and Ricardo; they had a million reasons to hate Spike-- most of them crisp and green, with pictures of dead presidents on them. They blamed him for the band's implosion and spectacular crash to the bottom that left them as broke as when they started. People say it takes only ten minutes to get used to a luxury, but a lifetime to get over losing it. Lucky for the Zombies they were always stoned, so their memories of the good life were too hazy to be painful.

Fast-forward three weeks to the present where Spike, still dead of course, has somehow taken over my life, causing me to put my house on the line, my reputation at risk and my sanity over the edge. Well, let's face it, I wasn't all that stable to begin with, but still...

It's hard to know where to start, but here goes. My name is Jamie Quinn. Jamie isn't short for anything; my mom just thought it was a good name, one that offered more opportunities than say Courtney or Brittany. She didn't want to burden me with society's stereotypes by choosing a name that was too girly, or sounded like a playboy bunny. She was always thinking ahead like that, which also made her a great nurse. Because she could connect the dots faster than anyone, she always knew when a patient was about to take a turn for the worse. Her co-workers at Hollywood Memorial Hospital (one of the top hospitals in Florida) were so impressed that they started calling her "Psychic Sue." Although she brushed it off whenever they did that, I think she was proud of her nickname. It was her super power, she would say. Superman may have had x-ray vision, but he could never match her diagnostic skills.

Unfortunately, like any super power, my mom's could be used for good or evil. And there were secrets behind those green eyes. When her cancer came back, she was the first to know, but she kept it to herself until it was too late for treatment. I'm sure she had her reasons, but I can't think of a single one that makes any sense. As usual, she had planned ahead. Her life insurance paid off the small house I grew up in on Polk Street and left me with enough cash to take some time off and gather my thoughts. The thought-gathering was her idea. Now, six months later, I am still trying to gather them, but it's no use. They are shadow puppets, gray wisps flitting through my brain, and they refuse to be caught. Somehow my mother knew that after she was gone I, too, would take a turn for the worse. Psychic Sue strikes again.

There is another thing you need to know about me--I'm a terrible sleeper. Let me put it this way, if I were taking a class in sleeping, I would get an 'F' (with an 'A' for effort, which doesn't count). But don't think I'm throwing a pity party for myself--I'm not. This is all relevant to the story. Because I don't sleep much, I wander the house at night like the ghost of Hamlet's father (also named Hamlet, of course), but I am much quieter about it. I rattle no chains and make no demands of anyone. I do, however, need to sleep later in the day than most people, just to catch up, which I am able to do now that I'm not working. I'm only telling you this so you'll understand how I slept through my Aunt Peg's call and her hysterical message on my answering machine.

It was Monday, July 1st, the day that Spike (newly dead) took over my life. I had staggered out of bed around eleven (a.m.) after a particularly rough night (although it's getting harder to rank them at this point), so it wasn't until my second cup of coffee that I noticed the blinking light on the phone. Hardly anyone calls me on my landline anymore, so I figured it was just a telemarketer or someone conducting a survey. When I finally gave in and pushed the button, the ragged sound of my Aunt Peg crying made me spill my coffee all over my lap. What she said sent my adrenaline level spiking to new levels.

"Oh my God, Jamie, where are you? I can't find your cell number...I don't know what to do. I need your help...Adam's in trouble (she's sobbing at this point and I can't understand what she's saying) he's....he's... been arrested! I'm so scared. Please call me the minute you hear this..."

Now I was officially freaked out. First, because my aunt sounds so much like my mother on the phone. Second, because my cousin Adam is not someone who should be in jail, *ever*. And third, because how could anyone expect *me* to help with a crisis of this magnitude? I could barely take care of myself!

There's one more thing I should tell you about myself, but I don't like to bring it up. Since I have no choice, I'll just throw it out there and hope you don't think less of me, or make assumptions about my honesty or integrity. The truth is...I'm a lawyer. There, I said it. I hope that hasn't changed your opinion of me. I practice family law exclusively, which means that my limited area of expertise includes divorce, adoption, paternity, custody and child support. I use the word 'limited' because it's the only area I know, and it's hard enough to keep up with that. The problem is that friends, family, acquaintances, and even strangers tend to ask my advice in areas that I know nothing about. I'm truly sorry, but I can't help you with a real estate closing, or tell you what your back injury is worth; I can't help you file your Social Security claim, or advise you whether to file for bankruptcy. And I sure as hell can't represent you in a criminal case.

For Adam's sake, I hoped that wasn't what my aunt had in mind.

By the time I called her back, Aunt Peg had gone from hysterical to eerily calm and I don't know which one worried me more. She said that they were at the Hollywood police station where Adam was being held. She needed to stay with him, so she couldn't talk, but she'd fill me in when I came down.

"I'll get down there as soon as I can," I said. "You guys hang in there, okay?" I wanted to sound reassuring, but I'm not exactly the cavalry.

"I'll try, Jamie," she said, her voice cracking. "But there's something else I need you to do..."

"Of course, Aunt Peg, what is it?"

"Can you please come dressed like a lawyer?"

∼

What scared me the most, starting out as a new lawyer, was that I couldn't begin to fathom the depths of my ignorance. The more I learned, the more I realized how much I didn't know. I've heard law schools actually teach students how to practice law these days, and not just about research and writing. Well, it's about damn time, I say. Now that I've been practicing law for ten years, I know what to do and where to stand, how to dress and how to negotiate and, if I'm not sure about something, I can usually bluff my way through. I've also learned how to size up my opponents: the nervous ones with shaky hands, the blustery ones with something to prove, and the cool, confident ones I longed to emulate. But, as my first boss used to say, half the battle is just showing up. The other half is preparing the best you can with the information you have.

In this instance, I had no information to go on except what I already knew about Adam's situation. I sat down at my computer to find the statute I needed and quickly printed a copy of it, along with the amendments. Then, looking in the mirror, I adjusted the lapel of my navy blue "power suit." After putting on my mother's elegant gold necklace, I touched up my hair and make-up and finished by dusting off my briefcase. My ensemble was complete. If I weren't already a lawyer, I could have easily played one on TV.

I couldn't remember the last time I'd left the house, but it had to be at least a week. The days all blurred together. It turns out that when you aren't working, it doesn't really matter what day it is. After grabbing my umbrella from its perch by the front door, I slid behind the wheel of my Mini Cooper. There was no need to check the weather, summer days are always the same here--hot and muggy in the morning, thunderstorms in the afternoon.

When you think about south Florida (and how can you avoid it when we're always in the news?) you probably think of trendy South Beach or swanky Palm Beach, where Donald Trump has a mansion; you may even think of Fort Lauderdale, where Spring Breakers used to swarm the beaches in drunken hordes until they were chased away, but you probably never think of Hollywood, the quiet town that lies between Miami and Fort Lauderdale. With an area of only thirty square miles, Hollywood is unpretentious, affordable and quaint. The streets are named for presidents, admirals and generals, which can turn a trip to the grocery store into an American history lesson. I suppose GPS has taken all the fun out of that. It's strange how technology enhances life and diminishes it at the same time.

I find living in Hollywood comforting, not only because I grew up here, but also because it doesn't change much. I can relive my favorite memories as I drive past my favorite landmarks--the Wings 'N' Curls restaurant where we used to meet after high school football games; and Stratford's Bar, where we went for billiards and cheap beer in college. If you're lucky enough to live and work in Hollywood, there's no such thing as a commute; everything is close by. Case in point, it's only four miles from my house on Polk Street to the Hollywood Police Station, but I still took the back streets to avoid the traffic lights. I would be arriving all too soon as it was and the thought of Adam--poor defenseless Adam--under arrest was twisting my stomach into knots. All the other times I hadn't been there for him were now prickling in my brain. I needed to focus if I was going to help him.

I arrived just minutes later and found a shady spot to park, but didn't turn off the car. I was feeling a little panicky, I must admit. Ten years as a lawyer and what did 1 know about criminal law? Only what I'd learned from watching a *Law and Order* marathon one Sunday--and I'd slept through most of it. In other words, nothing. Although the AC was blowing ice cold, beads of sweat dotted my upper lip and my hands were starting to feel clammy. Before I started sweating all over my best silk shirt, I decided to call my friend Grace. She'd know what to do. Grace was in-house counsel for a large securities firm, but she'd been a public defender right out of school. The call went straight to voice mail and my heart sank. I'd have to go in blind, what choice did I have? I felt my pulse throbbing in my left temple as I took a few calming breaths and turned off the ignition. Just as I was psyching myself up to get out of the car, my phone beeped. A text from Grace! Technology to the rescue! I take back everything I said before. With a sigh of relief, I turned the car back on and studied my phone with an intensity I usually reserve for pictures of Hugh Jackman.

Hey J--I'm stuck in a meeting, you ok?

Not so good, Gracie - my cousin Adam's been arrested!

OMG! What the hell happened???

No idea...I'm about to walk into Hollywood police station. Need your help, I'm clueless!

Ok, let's make a plan--if he's been charged, call me ASAP, and don't let him talk to anybody.

It might be too late...

True. The State attny could push for a psych eval but you'll hv to fight that or they can hold him 72 hrs.

Oh God, that's the last thing Adam needs!

Exactly. Now, if they don't charge him, you're golden. Just use the right buzz words & you'll hv a get out of jail free card. I'll send you the link now...

Gracie, you're the best!

Yeah, I know. Call me later.

Will do. Wish me luck...

As I crossed the short distance from the parking lot to the front door, the asphalt shimmered in the midday heat, creating watery mirages that popped in and out of existence. Towering palm trees loomed over me like self-appointed sentinels. (To be honest, I've been leery of tall palm trees ever since the day I almost got brained by a humongous palm frond falling from thirty feet up. Right in front of the courthouse! Talk about a personal injury case waiting to happen. The witnesses would've all been lawyers, except for that one lucky guy (or girl) that I (or my estate) hired to take the case. What a slam dunk that would've been. But what a stupid way to die, right?)

Although I'd driven by the police station hundreds of times on my way to court, I'd never been inside. In fact, I'd never been inside *any* police station--why would I?--and I had no idea what to expect. Maybe the hours I'd spent watching *Castle* and *The Mentalist* had prepared me for the real thing, but I had my doubts.

I guess I was expecting to walk through a metal detector, since that's the drill at the courthouse, but that wasn't the case. Instead, I found myself in a small lobby jam-packed with unhappy people. It was a zoo. On one side, a distraught woman with a screaming baby was crying to a female officer while, just a few feet away, two scruffy-looking men were in each other's faces, yelling about a broken lawn mower. At least I think that's what they were fighting about. I had to push my way through to reach the receptionist, who was safely ensconced behind bullet-proof glass. She was a bored twenty-something with magenta hair who barely looked up from her computer to acknowledge me. She seemed immune to the commotion in the lobby. It could have been happening in another dimension, or on a distant planet.

"You an attorney, ma'am?" she asked.

"Yes, I'm here for Adam Muller. I believe he's in custody."

"I'll need to see your Florida Bar card and ID. Are you carrying any firearms or weapons of any kind?"

"No, I most definitely am not." *When did my hometown turn into the O.K. Corral?*

After a cursory glance at my ID cards, she dismissed me with a nod. "Second door on the right," she said, buzzing me in with a flick of her long purple fingernail.

As I pulled the door open, I glanced back at the lawnmower guys who were now cursing each other out in what sounded like Russian. An officer built like a linebacker was heading their way and he looked grim. Keeping the peace seemed like a messy business. In fact, I thought it looked like the worst babysitting gig ever.

The contrast between the lobby and the other side of the door was remarkable. One little step had taken me from chaos to a well-ordered universe where everyone had a purpose and a destination. All around me, uniformed police officers and civilians were bustling about, some carrying folders, others having quick discussions in the hallway. If the lobby resembled an anthill that had been kicked over, then the inner office was a humming beehive. Alas, I must report that it looked nothing like the set of *Castle* or *The Mentalist*. How disappointing. I knew my day would be going downhill from there...

The second door on the right wasn't marked, so I knocked lightly before I opened it a crack. A shrill but familiar voice immediately pierced the silence.

"Leave us alone! My son has rights!!"

"Calm down, Aunt Peg, it's me," I said, as I slipped quietly into the room, closing the door behind me.

"Oh, Jamie, thank God you're here!" she said before she collapsed into my arms, sobbing.

I patted her on the back and made soothing noises while I glanced around the stark room. The blue Berber carpeting was new and the walls were freshly painted, but there were no decorations or pictures to break up the startling whiteness. In the center of the room was a small round table with four modular chairs and, curled up in a corner, hugging his knees and rocking back and forth, was my cousin Adam.

CHAPTER 2

"Can you *please* tell me what's going on?" I asked.

My aunt and I were sitting at the table, not talking, despite my best efforts. Adam was still in the corner, shutting out the world just like he did when he was a kid--before intensive therapy and an obsession with music helped him learn to cope. He would come around when he was ready. Until then, it was best to leave him alone. Poor Aunt Peg looked so haggard; it was as if twenty-two years of safeguarding Adam had finally done her in. Not even when she and Dave were divorcing, their marriage collapsing under the strain of caring for Adam, had she looked this defeated. She was only forty-two, but she looked sixty-two at that moment, with bags under her eyes and deep wrinkles on her forehead. I watched her pick up a paper clip from the table, twisting and untwisting it until it finally broke. She looked up at me.

"Jamie, I want to wake up from this nightmare, but I can't! It all started this morning...I dropped Adam off at his music lesson, like I always do. He's been taking drum lessons at the music store on Harrison Street. When I went to pick him up an hour later, there were police cars and an ambulance blocking the road. I almost crashed the car I was so terrified--I thought something had happened to Adam! Any mother would've panicked, but it was worse for me because of Adam. He doesn't see trouble coming. He's too trusting, even after what happened with those horrible kids..."

She started crying again and I dug a tissue out of my purse. Divorce lawyers always have tissues handy.

"Then what happened, Aunt Peg?" I couldn't imagine where this story was going.

"I stopped a policeman--it was more like I grabbed him--and demanded to know what was going on. He said there had been a homicide! I started crying and screaming for Adam and then... he...he said...Adam wasn't hurt, but they were taking him into custody!"

She was on the verge of hysteria, so she closed

her eyes and took a few deep breaths. I'd seen Adam use this calming technique before.

I waited a minute and then gently prodded her, "Aunt Peg?"

She continued as if she were in a trance. "I followed the police car back to the station. At first, they weren't going to let me in here because Adam is over eighteen but, when they saw him like this, they changed their minds." She stopped and looked at Adam with tears in her eyes.

"Margaret Muller, look at me!" I snapped.

"What, Jamie?"

"Will you tell me who died already?"

"I'm sorry, I thought I told you--it was Adam's music teacher, Spike. One of the other teachers heard a scream and ran into the room. He saw Adam standing over Spike's body. And he had blood on his hands..."

I jumped up from my chair. "Oh my God, that's terrible! But Adam must've found him like that, right?"

"That's what I said, but they arrested him anyway!" She buried her face in her hands.

I felt the room closing in on me. The air was so stifling I thought I would pass out. This was way worse than anything I could've imagined. *Think, Jamie, think!* Whenever I have a crisis, I try to put things in perspective by asking myself: *If I screw this up, is anybody going to die?* Usually, the answer is no...

Grace would be able to fix this, I was sure of it, but I needed more information. I started pacing back and forth, wearing a path in the new carpeting.

"Aunt Peg, we're going to get through this, okay?" I put my arm around her shoulders, it was only a half-hug, but it seemed to do the trick. She nodded.

"Tell me what happened since you got here, has Adam said anything?"

"Not a word."

"Has anyone come in to talk to you?"

"Yes, a Detective Hernandez and a young man in a suit. I told them our attorney was on her way. I'm supposed to tell them when you get here."

I decided it was a good time to take out my phone and read the information Grace had sent. Talk about your crash course in criminal law! I was so far out of my comfort zone I didn't think I'd ever find my way back. I remembered the statute I had in my briefcase (it was the only thing in there, aside from a legal pad) and took it out. I told my aunt to stay put, I was going to find Detective Hernandez.

"One more thing," I said, "and this is really important. Pretend we are not related. It's better if they don't think I have a stake in this, okay?"

"Alright, but what should I call you? Miss Quinn?"

"Actually, I prefer 'your highness' or 'my royal lady,' but you can call me Jamie. Just for today." I laughed and kissed her on the cheek. In return, she squeezed my hand and gave me a weak smile. It seemed like a fair trade.

CHAPTER 3

I was making my way down the hall when someone tapped me on the shoulder.

"Excuse me, are you Jamie Quinn?"

I turned around and found myself face to face with a GQ cover model. From his shiny wingtip shoes to his tailored Armani suit to his glossy black hair, this guy looked like he was going places--if he hadn't already arrived. I was pretty sure he was not Detective Hernandez.

"I see my reputation precedes me," I said with a smile. "And you are?"

"Nick Dimitropoulos, State Attorney's office." He shook my hand firmly but briefly, all business.

"I've been assigned to the homicide case from this morning. Are you representing Adam Muller?"

He tried to sound nonchalant, but I could tell he was stoked, like a lion circling a herd of wildebeests. Well, this guy was messing with the wrong wildebeest.

"I am." *Did those two words really just come out of my mouth?*

"And what firm did you say you're with?" he asked, eyeing my two year old suit, purchased off the rack at Macy's. As my mother used to say, the classics never go out of style.

I smiled sweetly. Only rookie lawyers judge you by your appearance. I stored that tidbit of information in my brain. "I'm a sole practitioner, my office is downtown. So, jumping ahead a little, have you charged my client with anything?"

Before he could answer, one of his assistants walked over and whispered something in his ear. She handed him some paperwork and then left. Nick (I was sure he wouldn't mind if I called him Nick) glanced at it and frowned. Turning his attention back to me without so much as an apology, he said:

"Not yet, but we're working on it."

"Do you have any evidence, besides the fact that he wandered into a murder scene? Being in the wrong place at the wrong time isn't a crime, as far as I know."

He looked disdainful. "Then, Ms. Quinn, you

don't know much. Your client made several incriminating statements."

I was so angry I could hardly contain myself. "You spoke to my client without me present? After he told you he had an attorney?"

"Of course not. He hasn't said a word since he was brought in, and nobody asked him anything. But he did make spontaneous utterances at the scene."

Skimming the papers in his hand, he said, "It's in the report. I'll read it to you:

Victim deceased, apparently from blunt force trauma. Suspect found standing next to victim. When undersigned approached the suspect, suspect made the following unsolicited statements: 'It's all my fault, I did a bad thing,' and also: 'I'm sorry, I'm sorry, I'm so sorry...'"

Oh, Adam! How was I ever going to talk my way out of this? I would have to go all alpha dog on Mr. State Attorney.

"Listen, Nick," I said, "I know how that sounds, but here's the story. My client says *all kinds of things* because he has Asperger's Syndrome. Are you familiar with it? No? Well, you might want to read up on it. People with Asperger's Syndrome have difficulties with social interaction and often display unusual behaviors. The bottom line is this-- Adam Muller is protected under the Americans with Disabilities Amendments Act of 2008. Here's a copy of the statute. So, if you're not going to charge him, you have to let him go. Immediately. Or we'll be filing a claim against the department under the ADA."

His expression was a mix of contempt and barely-controlled anger. I must say it took away from his chiseled good looks, all that venom. When he was through glaring at me, he turned and walked off without so much as a "nice to meet ya." What's up with people's manners these days? I blame it all on the internet.

I yelled after him, "I'm entitled to a copy of the police report."

He turned around and walked back over to me. "Listen, Quinn," he said, coldly, "I know your guy did it and when we're through analyzing the evidence, there will be charges. Try hiding behind your statute then."

He stormed off again and, this time, he didn't come back. Man, what a sore loser! He probably wouldn't have been a gracious winner, either. I took a deep breath and shook the tension out of my neck and shoulders. Unclenching my jaw would take a bit longer. *You can relax, Jamie,* I thought, *Adam is safe. At least for now....*

CHAPTER 4

"I've never been so glad to get home in my life!" Aunt Peg said, throwing her purse on the dining room table and kicking off her shoes. "I'm exhausted."

"You and me both, sister," I said, collapsing into a comfy recliner in the corner.

No sooner had I sat down than two exuberant puppies jumped in my lap and started licking my face non-stop.

"And who do we have here, Adam?" I smiled at my cousin, who was sitting on the floor next to my chair, petting the dogs.

"The black one is Angus Young, he's a Scottish terrier and he's six months old. The reddish one is

Bono and he's an Irish setter. He's only three months old."

"I'm sensing a theme here..." I laughed as I watched Adam roll around on the floor with the puppies. He looked like an overgrown puppy himself. I couldn't think of a dog breed with blond curly hair like Adam's, but if it existed, that's what he'd be.

Aunt Peg brought me a glass of iced tea and an orange juice for Adam. Then she sat down on the sofa and propped her feet up on the coffee table.

"You know, Adam, I don't think I told you this before," she said, "but I took Jamie to a U2 concert when she was sixteen."

Adam's mouth dropped open, his brown eyes wide. "Wow! I wish I could've gone."

"I tell you what," I said. "If AC/DC or U2 perform in south Florida again, I'll take you."

"That's awesome, Jamie! I can't wait! Can I show you the music stuff in my room now?" he asked, trying to pull me out of the chair. He was hard to resist since he outweighed me by at least fifty pounds. Nobody would ever guess we were cousins because he was tall and fair and I was short and olive-skinned. I'm told I take after my father's side, but I wouldn't know.

"Sure, Adam, but I need to talk to your mom first, okay?"

"Why don't you take the dogs for a walk, sweetheart? They haven't been out all day," Aunt Peg said.

After Adam bounded out the door, I sat down next to Aunt Peg and gulped my iced tea like a person who had just crossed the Sahara. I didn't even give the ice a chance to melt. My aunt jumped up to refill my glass.

"I can't remember the last time I was here," I said, making conversation while she fussed in the kitchen.

To my surprise, Aunt Peg burst into tears. I rushed over to comfort her.

"It's been a rough day, I know," I said, patting her shoulder.

She pulled me into a tight hug.

"Oh, Jamie, I'm so sorry, I haven't been there for you at all. Since Sue died, I've been such a mess, I could barely function. It's all I could do to make myself go to work and take care of Adam. Sue wasn't just my big sister, she was my best friend...and I can't believe she's gone."

Then we were both crying. Me, because I hadn't thought about anyone else's grief except my own. I had to be the most selfish, self-absorbed person on the planet.

"I wasn't there for you either, Aunt Peg, and I'm sorry." I grabbed a tissue out of my purse and blew my nose. "What would my mom say if she saw the two of us crying like this, with mascara running down our faces?"

My aunt smiled through her tears. "She'd say 'guilt is a stupid waste of time. If you feel bad, get off your butt and do something about it.'"

"Exactly. So, you and I are officially giving up on the guilt trips, okay? Personally, I'd rather take a trip to just about anywhere else." We walked back to the living room together and sat down on the sofa.

"Deal," she said. "And thank-you so much for today, I don't know how you convinced them to let Adam go. You're amazing!"

"And I don't know how you got Adam out of his meltdown! It was like magic."

She laughed. "I have years of experience! Actually, all I had to do was tell him we were going home and the dogs were waiting for him. But I did set up an emergency appointment with his therapist for tomorrow, he definitely needs that. And I should probably make an appointment for myself, too. I'm so glad this nightmare is over."

I couldn't tell her the truth, but she'd find out soon enough. It wasn't over. It was just getting started...

CHAPTER 5

Exactly one week later, I was having dinner with Grace at my favorite birthday restaurant, Le Bonne Crepe, in Fort Lauderdale. Except that it wasn't my birthday. We'd picked it because it's next-door to Grace's office on upscale Las Olas Boulevard. (I mentioned that she works for a big securities firm, right?) Also, I knew she had bad news for me and I felt that I deserved a treat, like a prisoner's last meal.

"How about Crêpe Suzette?" Grace said. "When they light it on fire, it's like dinner *and* a show. Not to mention it's scrumptious." Grace always got excited about dessert.

"Are you kidding?" I said. "That's the reason I

come here. I *love* Grand Marnier. Crêpe Suzette is an after-dinner drink disguised as dessert."

"Vanilla ice cream on the side?"

"Do you really have to ask?"

She laughed. "Just testing you. So, should we get to work now?"

"You're ruining my dessert buzz, Gracie!" I said, throwing up my hands.

"Okay, okay, sorry James, it can wait..."

After we had eaten every bite, licked our fingers *and* the forks, we sat back in our upholstered chairs and sipped our coffee, soaking up the cozy ambience of the French Bistro.

"I would've licked the plate if you weren't here..." Grace said, wistfully.

"You know I don't judge."

"See? That's why I like you," she said with a laugh.

∼

Grace and I had been friends since our second year at Nova Law School when we discovered we were in all the same classes. It turns out when you run into a person four times a day, every day, eventually you'll strike up a conversation. Grace was motivated, one of those people who actually wanted to be a lawyer, serious about school, but with a crazy sense of humor. I was an English Lit major who had drifted into law school for lack of a better plan. Being friends with Grace made law school so much better.

One night, we were at Grace's apartment studying for a Torts exam. Around three in the morning, we started getting punchy. We'd just finished reading about the "eggshell plaintiff" (someone more susceptible to injury than the average person) when Grace darted off to the kitchen. She came back a few minutes later holding a plate and giggling her head off. On the plate was a little person she'd made out of eggshells with the words "Help me Jamie!" in ketchup next to it. I almost fell out of my chair laughing.

"Grace, you 'crack' me up!" I said, feeling quite witty. Of course, at three a.m., my standards tend to drop considerably.

The next day, during the exam, all I could think about was Grace's poor little eggshell person and I had to stifle my giggles. Everyone in the room must've thought I was nuts.

∼

"Jamie, it's that time, I'm afraid..." Grace looked serious.

"I guess I'm ready." I said, leaning forward. I

pulled a pad of paper and pen from my purse and laid them on the table.

"Do you want the bad news, or the really bad news?"

"Is 'neither' an acceptable answer?" I sighed. "Whatever you think, Grace."

She signaled the waiter for the check, which he promptly deposited in the center of the table.

"Okay, I reviewed the police report and the forensics report from the crime scene. You already know about the incriminating statements Adam made, but there's more. The victim's blood was found on Adam's shoes, but only on the soles, which could have happened when he walked over to the body." She paused to look at her notes. "Moving on to cause of death, the victim, Spike, who doesn't seem to have a last name, was killed by a blow to the head. The murder weapon was a didgeridoo, which was found at the scene."

"What the hell is a did-ger-i-doo?"

"I had to look it up. According to Wikipedia, it's an Australian Aboriginal wind instrument. Basically, it's a long wooden tube around four feet long that can weigh up to ten pounds. This one weighed six. According to the report, there were several sets of fingerprints on it, including the victim's." Grace looked at me sympathetically. "And Adam's..."

I groaned. "Just because he touched the didgeriwhatever doesn't mean he murdered his music teacher! He plays lots of musical instruments, that's his thing. And Adam would never hurt anyone, even if they were pounding him senseless. Remember when he was in middle school and those kids beat him up and broke his arm? He couldn't even defend himself! He had no reason to hurt his teacher."

Grace nodded, her long dark hair falling into her face. "I know, Jamie."

"Well, what news could be worse than that?"

"The State Attorney plans to press charges against Adam next week."

"Damn it!" I slammed my pad of paper on the table. "Have they even looked for the real murderer? Someone with a reason to kill this guy?"

"It doesn't seem like. Their golden boy, Nick Dimitropoulos, is handling the case. He's a hotshot right out of school who wants to make a name for himself. I hear he's planning to go into politics, like his father..."

"Oh my God! Don't tell me he's Theo Dimitropoulos' son! That's just great--the son of a state senator is gunning for my disabled cousin..." I felt like crying, or screaming, or both simultaneously. "What am I going to do, Grace? I can't represent him, and my aunt doesn't have the money to hire a lawyer. She's an elementary school teacher."

Grace looked thoughtful. "What about Adam's father?"

"Dave?" I shook my head. "No way, he's broke. He isn't even part of Adam's life anymore. He got remarried and moved out of state. I think he has three more kids."

"Well, here's my advice: let the public defender represent him. This is a high-profile case, so they'll put their best person on it, and that's Susan Doyle. She's very good and she's been at this a lot longer than 'Slick Nick'. We used to work together at the PD's office and she won't mind if I help her strategize. You know I'll do whatever I can for you..."

I felt a glimmer of hope. "What if I mortgaged my house? It's free and clear. Then I could hire a great defense attorney--nothing against Susan, of course."

Grace shook her head. "That won't work," she said gently. "You can't qualify for a mortgage because you're not employed. And you may need to use your house as collateral."

"Collateral? For what?" I asked.

"To post bail, Jamie," she said.

CHAPTER 6

It had been a long weekend and Grace had given me a lot to think about. Too much, in fact. Trying to keep myself from curling into the fetal position was a challenge, but I needed to stay upbeat for Aunt Peg. She had no idea what was coming, and I wasn't ready to tell her yet. The only thing keeping me sane was focusing on Adam and preparing for the ordeal to come. And so, first thing Monday morning, I made a phone call.

"Susan Doyle speaking."

The voice on the phone was confident, authoritative. She had a tone that said, 'This better be important, I have no time for nonsense.' She'd only said three words and I liked her already.

"Hello, this is Jamie Quinn, I'm Grace Anderson's friend..."

"Oh yes, Miss Quinn, I've been expecting your call. Grace told me about your cousin's situation. Unfortunately, it looks like the case is moving forward. On a personal note, I'm appalled that the state attorney has decided to prosecute with only circumstantial evidence and no apparent motive, but he's under a lot of pressure to put someone behind bars. Not to mention, there's a lot of publicity to be had," she added wryly.

"So I've heard," I said, feeling my jaw tighten. "I wanted to touch base with you for a few reasons. First, I'd like to know what to expect. My cousin may be twenty-two, but emotionally and socially, he's much younger. Adam is a gentle boy and he'd never hurt anyone; he's just not capable of it. With his Asperger's, he can't handle stress and I'm afraid this is going to destroy him..." I started crying, like I knew I would, and walked over to the kitchen sink to splash water on my face. I had to get a grip.

"I understand, Miss Quinn--Jamie--and I've been thinking about that. Adam will have to go through arrest and booking, but there are some things we can do for him. The state attorney will want a flashy arrest, but we can avoid that if Adam agrees to turn himself in. In addition, because of his Asperger's, I can ask the judge to appoint an attorney ad litem to protect him. Finally, I can ensure that Adam goes straight to court for his initial appearance, without spending any time in jail."

I breathed a sigh of relief--no jail! "How will you do that?"

"I think the state attorney will agree it would hurt his case if Adam had a breakdown in jail and ended up in a psychiatric hospital."

"I'm so glad you're on our side!" I said. "What will happen at the hearing?"

"The judge will determine if there's probable cause for the arrest. If the answer is yes, then he or she will appoint the public defender and set bail."

"That was my next question. How much would the bail be?" I was pacing back and forth between the kitchen and the living room.

"Hard to say. Your cousin certainly isn't a flight risk, but this is a capital crime and it's also a political hot potato. I'll do my best, but I can't make any promises."

"I understand. Just so you know, I'll be the one posting bail. What happens after that?" I had stopped pacing. Now I was chewing my nails.

"An arraignment hearing is usually held within 21 days of the first appearance. At that hearing, Adam will plead not guilty. The judge can revisit the bail at that time. Next, the state attorney reviews the case and decides if there is enough evidence to proceed. If they find enough evidence, then Adam will be formally charged. This must happen within 175 days of arrest." I could hear her talking to someone in the background.

"Thank-you so much. I don't want to take any more of your time, but please tell me what I can do to help...I'll do anything. I'll even make your coffee and sharpen your pencils."

Susan laughed. "What a great offer! Not necessary though. There *is* something important you can do, if it's within your means. We're on a tight budget over here. If you could hire a private investigator to dig around for information, it might make all the difference. You'll need one willing to stretch the rules, but you didn't hear that from me."

"Of course I'll do it! What kind of information do you need?"

"How about I e-mail you a list later today?" she said.

"Perfect! I can't thank you enough." I said, starting to tear up.

"So much appreciation and I haven't even done anything yet," she said with a laugh. "We'll talk soon, Jamie."

The smile left my face as soon as I hung up. Where was I going to find a dirty private investigator?

CHAPTER 7

True to her word, Susan Doyle e-mailed me the list a few hours later. It was three pages of questions that seemed impossible to answer. I felt as panicky as when I was in law school and dreamt I had a test I hadn't studied for, in a class I'd never been to.

Studying the list, I wondered how anyone, even a sleazy PI, could uncover some of these facts, like whether Spike had enemies, or whether he'd been in any arguments the week of his murder. I took a deep breath and looked at it again. There were actually a few questions I could answer myself, using public records. Before tackling this online scavenger hunt, I would make myself some coffee to ensure maximum alertness. Since I hardly slept anyway, one more cup wouldn't matter.

After sweeping the bills and my mom's estate papers off the desk, I sat down at my computer and pulled up the site for Florida Secretary of State Corporations. I decided to start there. Under 'corporate entities', I typed in "The Screaming Zombie," which was the name of the music store. Although I'd seen the store on Harrison Street many times, I'd always assumed it was a bar. When nothing popped up, I typed the name "Spike" under corporate officers and got a hit: "Spike Enterprises, Inc. d/b/a/ The Screaming Zombie." Spike was listed as the director. The only other officer was the treasurer, Marian Wolinsky. *Need to find Marian Wolinsky* I wrote on a legal pad.

I decided to pull up the music store's website and typed in: *The Screaming Zombie.* To my surprise, I got dozens of hits. Who knew *The Screaming Zombies* was the name of a heavy metal band? Apparently, everyone in the world did, except for me. I found online fan clubs and chat boards, as well as YouTube videos and downloadable songs. I even found a chart ranking the greatest drummers of all time, and Spike was one of them. At least now I understood the name of the store. Although *The Screaming Zombies* broke up in 2001, they still had many devoted fans, all of them heavily tattooed and pierced. I watched a video of the Zombies performing on You Tube and then watched an interview with Spike, which spooked me a little. While I never speak ill of the dead (at least I never have before), I will make an exception for Spike. After watching his interview, I was able to draw certain conclusions: 1) he was stoned; 2) he was an egomaniac; 3) he was a legend in his own mind; and 4) he was nasty and mean. He did say one interesting thing though: every time he went on a drinking binge, he brought home a new German shepherd. By the looks of him, he must have had quite a collection...

Next up, the actual website for the music store, where I found lots of information. I saw that they sold a wide array of instruments, and provided lessons for even more. The only instrument I didn't see listed in either category was the didgeridoo. I made a note on my pad. *Whose didgeridoo was it?* Next, I clicked on the 'Meet Our Instructors' link and hit the jackpot. All four instructors were listed (including Spike), with the instruments they taught and their photographs. I printed the page and made a note to Google each instructor later. I moved on to the 'About Us' section, which should have been called, "About Spike," because all five pages paid homage to him. Reading that, you'd think Spike was the greatest drummer ever born; that he'd been the star of the "The Screaming Zombies", and that the city of Hollywood should be grateful he chose to live there.

I must've dozed off for a minute with my head on the desk, because the next thing I knew my cellphone was ringing next to my ear. My ringtone is Vivaldi's violin concerto, *Spring*, and I was dreaming I was at the symphony with my mom. I woke up and fumbled with the phone.

"Hello?"

"Jamie, were you sleeping? I'm so sorry."

"It's alright, Aunt Peg..." I was still disoriented. It had been such a lovely dream...

"I hate to bother you, but..."

I sat up, suddenly wide wake. "What's wrong?

"Adam isn't doing well, he's having nightmares and he's barely eating. He's refusing to do his homework, or even play any music. His therapist started him on anti-anxiety medication, but it isn't working. He thinks we should try hypnotherapy to help Adam get past his traumatic experience." My aunt sounded exhausted and worried.

"Can you give the therapist permission to speak with me?" I had the beginning of an idea.

"Of course I will," she said, "but Jamie, I had another reason for calling. They were talking about the murder on the 11:00 news. They said Spike was killed with a didgeridoo..."

"I heard that, too."

"Jamie, I don't know how much more of this I can take!" Aunt Peg was crying into the phone.

"I don't understand," I said.

"The didgeridoo--they showed a picture of it. It was Adam's."

CHAPTER 8

THINGS JUST KEPT GETTING WORSE AND ALL I wanted was to go back to my imaginary symphony. Was that so much to ask?

Now, I know I should've told my aunt what was going on when I had the chance, but I couldn't do it. You might judge me for it--but you weren't there. When Margaret Muller says she can't take much more, she means it, and I didn't want to be the one to push her over the edge. Still, I needed to know how the didgeridoo ended up in Spike's office, so I eased into asking Aunt Peg about it. Her explanation made sense to me: Adam had been teaching himself to play, and wanted to show off for Spike, so he brought the didgeridoo to his lesson the week before. Unfortunately, I knew that my nemesis, Nick the state attorney, wouldn't see it that way at all. To him, it would be proof that Adam had planned the attack. I spent a few more minutes comforting my aunt and then wrapped up the call, promising to keep in touch.

Although it was after midnight, and officially Tuesday, I was too wired to even try to sleep, so I went back to my scavenger hunt. First, I googled the music teachers. There was a married couple, Steve and Rosa Michaels. Steve taught trumpet and saxophone, Rosa taught flute and piccolo. My search revealed they had been high school sweethearts at Hollywood Hills High, where they'd played in band together. How cute!

The only other teacher, aside from Spike, was Olga Gonzalez, who taught piano and guitar. Nothing came up on her. While I was at it, I figured I'd do a search for Marian Wolinsky, the treasurer of Spike's corporation. I found that she managed a fan site dedicated to Spike, in all of his awesomeness. There were photos of Marian and Spike together all over the site. Marian looked like a biker chick, leather vest, tight jeans, black boots, and lots of tattoos. In almost every picture, she was looking at Spike adoringly. I wonder how much he had to pay her to do that!

Next up, the Broward Clerk's website, to search for criminal and civil court records. Not surprisingly, Spike had over a dozen speeding tickets and other traffic-related offenses, as well as drug possession charges from way back. The civil records told another story: Spike and Spike Enterprises, Inc. (*d/b/a The Screaming Zombie*), were being sued by none other than Snake, Slasher and Slime, a/k/a Daryl, Marcus and Ricardo, a/k/a the rest of the Zombies! The suit was over Spike's use of the band's name for his store. The plaintiffs were accusing Spike and Spike Enterprises, Inc., of unjust enrichment, trademark infringement, etc. That sure sounded like bad blood to me, but was it a motive for murder? I made more notes on my legal pad.

While I was on the court website, I ran Spike's name through probate and found that someone had already opened an estate for him. Only the personal representative can open the estate, so I scrolled down to see who that was. Drum roll, please....it was... Marian Wolinsky! I definitely needed to have a chat with this lady. I also planned to visit the courthouse to read Spike's will. Since Spike's beneficiaries stood to profit from his death, I wanted to know who they were. My legal pad was filling up.

Finally, I ran criminal checks on all of the staff. Marian had some old possession charges, as well as a charge of disturbing the peace, hardly shocking. She and Spike must've been partying pretty hard that night.

Olga Gonzalez, the piano teacher, had no criminal record, but the high school sweethearts were another story. It turned out Rosa Michaels had filed domestic violence restraining orders against Steve on three separate occasions, but then dismissed them. The most recent one was obtained only two weeks before Spike's death, and she had filed for divorce at the same time. It could be nothing, it could be something, but Steve sounded like a man in need of an anger management class, or two...

I'd had enough, my brain was fried. To quote Miss Scarlett, tomorrow is another day. I fell into bed, in search of Vivaldi.

CHAPTER 9

I WOKE UP WAY TOO EARLY BECAUSE THE CAT, all twelve pounds of him, jumped on my head, yowling and demanding to be fed. He was always demanding something. I didn't mention that I have a cat before because I'm in denial. Mr. Paws was my mother's cat and I promised her I'd take care of him, even though we despised each other. That is, Mr. Paws and I despised each other, not my mother and I, just to clarify. Naturally, we don't get along any better now that it's just the two of us. I did take the liberty of changing his name from Mr. Paws to Mr. Pain in the Ass, but he never answers to anything anyway, except the sound of food being poured in his bowl.

After feeding his royal highness, I took a quick

shower and got dressed. I poured my coffee into a to-go cup and grabbed a granola bar before dashing out the door. As you can tell, I'm not big on breakfast. Before I fired up the old Mini Cooper, I texted Grace.

"Morning, Sunshine! I'll be at the main courthouse later, you free for lunch?"

"I wish! How about I meet you over there for a quick visit?"

"Great! Lots to tell you. What time?" I texted back.

"10.00? Cafeteria?"

"Perfect, see you there. I'll be the one with the black cloud over her head."

"I think I'll recognize you..."

The line to enter the courthouse was snaky and long, like it was most mornings. That's because all the judges schedule their motion calendars for 8:45 a.m. These non-evidentiary hearings are supposed to last only five minutes, but they never do, which causes crowds of people to spill into the hallways. It makes me feel claustrophobic and crabby. I knew it had to be a Tuesday because that's when the bearded preacher man with the wire glasses graces us with his presence. There he was, standing on his crate by the courthouse doors, yelling advice he got straight from Jesus. Deep sigh. I was in no mood to hear proselytizing...

I had no problem checking out Spike's probate file from the clerk. What I hoped to glean from the will was a clue that would point to someone other than Adam as the killer. But that didn't happen...

∼

"You're kidding me! I can't believe it. Tell me again what the will said," Grace was buttering her everything bagel. We were in the courthouse cafeteria and I was catching her up.

"You heard me. Spike left his entire estate to a German Shepherd Rescue organization. The only other bequest was that he left his dog, Beast, to Marian Wolinsky, with $10,000.00 for his care." I was shaking my head, amazed by Spike's generosity. Maybe he wasn't as big a jerk as I'd thought.

"Go figure!" Grace said. "So, that's pretty interesting stuff you found, that lawsuit the Zombies filed, and the music teacher with the domestic violence problem. What's your next step?"

"I have a million questions for Marian Wolinsky, so that meeting needs to happen. Also, I have to find a PI who walks on the dark side, according to my new best friend Susan Doyle, and I have no idea how to find one..."

"Jamie! I thought I was your best friend. I'm going to let that slide. Do you remember my favorite

Zen saying? You already have everything you need." Then she looked at me expectantly.

"What are you saying? That I know a dirty PI?" Maybe I was too tired to understand...then it came to me, like a flash. "Duke? You want me to call Duke Broussard? No way! He's a creep."

"Exactly!" Grace laughed. "And he owes you, big time. You saved his skin when you handled his divorce. Right?"

"Oh, my God! His wife was so furious when she caught him cheating on her--she reported him to the IRS, the Better Business Bureau, the PI licensing board, the newspapers, and Angie's List. She trashed him all over Facebook and Twitter too. Talk about a woman scorned!" I laughed.

"Didn't she also buy a billboard on I-95?" Grace glanced at her watch and started tidying the table.

"Yes, she did! I forgot about that. Not the bimbo he thought she was, huh? Don't worry, Grace, I'll clean up. You get back to work," I said.

She gave me a peck on the cheek and turned to go. "Call him, Jamie. You know I'm right."

"Yeah, you usually are." I said.

CHAPTER 10

When I got home, there were two messages blinking on my answering machine. When did I become so popular? I listened to them as I sorted the mail. The first was Aunt Peg leaving me the name and number of Adam's therapist, Dr. Simon. The other was Susan Doyle asking if Adam would be able to take a polygraph in the future. What perfect timing, what synchronicity! Dr. Simon was the one person who could answer Susan's question. Not to mention I had some questions of my own for the good doctor. At least I hoped he was a good doctor...

I needed something to go right, especially since Spike's will had been such a dead end (Jamie, this isn't the time to make bad jokes!) Time was not on my side, and the Rolling Stones' couldn't convince me otherwise. The more I thought about it, the more I was sure Spike's murder had been a crime of passion or opportunity. Nobody plans to kill with a didgeridoo, for heaven's sake, especially one that wasn't there a week earlier. It had to be a person with access to the store, or someone Spike knew, which narrowed the possibilities to the following:

1) A break-in gone bad, OR
2) One of the Zombies, OR
3) A teacher, OR
4) A student (parent of a student?) OR
5) Someone who hated Spike for a reason yet to be determined.

I suppose that's why Susan Doyle had sent me three pages of questions. Answer all of those, and you'll find your killer. Although Marian Wolinsky would have some of the answers, if I wanted to tackle the tough questions, I'd have to call him, the president of his own fan club, Duke Broussard.

CHAPTER 11

"Hello, Duke? This is--"

"Hey Darlin', what took you so long to call?" Duke was smooth. That's how he'd been married three times.

"Do you even know who this is?" I asked, laughing

"Of course I do, Darlin'. Jameson happens to be the name of my favorite whiskey *and* my favorite lawyer. I like to keep it simple. Besides, I have you on speed dial. You never know when you'll need your lawyer. I can't be huntin' for your number when I'm in jail, dead drunk, now can I?"

"Way to plan ahead, Duke," *Man, I hoped I never got that call.* "How have you been?"

"Life's grand! The only way I'd enjoy it more is if there were two of me." Duke could've been the poster boy for those 'Life is Good' shirts, except his stick figure would have a beer in its hand and a girl on either side. In fact, he was probably at a bar right now.

"Great! I knew you'd bounce back from your divorce." *Please let him remember the offer he made me.* I hate asking for favors.

He laughed. "I should thank Candy for putting my face on that billboard--I got so much business from that. And the ladies liked it too!"

I rolled my eyes. Lucky he couldn't see me.

"So, are you callin' to take me up on my offer?" he asked.

Yes! I jumped off my sofa and did a little dance. "As a matter of fact, I am," I said, trying to keep the excitement out of my voice.

"Sounds good to me, Darlin'. Why don't you meet me at *The Big Easy* on Harrison? They have blues music startin' at eight."

Of course Duke conducts his business from a bar! They probably hand out business cards for him, too.

"Okay," I said. "See you there. And thanks, Duke."

"You're welcome. You know, most of my dates

don't thank me 'til the end, if you catch my drift." I could almost see him leering through the phone.

"What? This isn't a date--"

But he'd already hung up.

CHAPTER 12

I DRESSED WITH CARE FOR MY 'APPOINTMENT' with Duke, opting for business casual, as if I were attending an event at the Broward Bar, instead of an actual bar. And forget about lipstick--wearing lipstick around Duke was like waving a red flag at a bull. You were just asking for trouble.

I arrived before eight and parked close by. I was definitely overdressed for the muggy summer weather, but it couldn't be helped. As I crossed the street, I saw Duke sitting outside at the bar, drinking a beer. Who knew, maybe he lived there? He looked the same as ever: sandy brown hair cut shoulder length, designer jeans and a white Tommy Bahama shirt unbuttoned to show off his shark tooth necklace. And of course, a tan, he always had a tan. I wondered if he was wearing his favorite alligator boots. I still don't believe he killed that alligator....As far as I could tell, he hadn't changed at all since I'd seen him a year ago. I wondered if I had.

As I walked toward the bar, Duke saw me and started grinning.

"Look at you Miss Jamie, all lawyered up! Do I have a court hearing I don't know about?"

"Not yet," I said with a smile, "but the night is young. Anything can happen."

"Ain't that the truth? Why don't you have a seat and we'll get you a cocktail." He patted the barstool next to him. And they say chivalry is dead.

"I'll have a Pinot Grigio," I said to the bartender, before turning my attention to Duke. "How's work, keeping you busy?"

He polished off his beer and ordered another one. "Come on, Jamie," he said, looking me in the eye. "You didn't call me out of the blue to ask me how's work, did you? What's going on, you in trouble?"

Just then, the band started up inside the restaurant and I stopped to listen. They were playing a Muddy Waters song, and they were pretty good. I really needed to get out more...

I sipped my wine. "Am I that transparent?"

"No, girl, I'm just a damn good PI!" He gave me

a wink and then laughed at his own joke. You can say that for Duke, he was easily amused.

"Okay, but before I tell you my long story that involves a heavy metal band, a murder, and a state attorney with political ambitions, I need to make one thing clear..."

Duke's green eyes were watching me closely, he loved a good story. "What's that, Darlin?"

"This is not a date."

CHAPTER 13

"Then I guess you won't mind if I check out the lovely ladies?" Duke said, with a leer.

I snorted. "Like you weren't going to do that anyway."

When the bartender pointed at my empty glass, I nodded. I figured what the hell-- this was my biggest night out in months, even if I was spending it with Duke Broussard.

"Just out of curiosity," I said, "On the phone earlier, what offer did you think I was accepting?"

Duke gave me a look. "The one where I said, 'Hey Jamie, let's you and me go out and celebrate, I finally got away from my crazy wife.' What'd you think I meant?"

"Oh, I remembered a different offer," I said.

"The one where you said, "Jamie, you rock! If you ever need my help for anything, just call.""

"Yeah, I vaguely remember that," he said.

"You'd remember more if you weren't always soaking your brain in booze," I teased.

"What fun would that be?" He laughed, showing off his perfect teeth. "Well, where's that story you promised me?"

And so, with blues riffs as my backdrop, I told Duke the tale of the music store murder and its oddball cast of characters. I explained what I'd learned so far and how, despite Adam's strange confession, and his fingerprints on the didgeridoo, I would stake my life on his innocence.

"Damn, Jamie! This sounds like a made-for-TV movie. Count me in. What do you need me to do?"

I'd been holding my breath waiting for Duke's reaction and I finally let it escape into a sigh of relief. I pulled out Susan Doyle's list of questions and we began to strategize. Duke would run background checks on Spike, the band and everyone who worked in the music store. If that didn't turn up anything, he would also check out the students and their parents. When he started telling me how he could get cell phone and bank records, I put my fingers in my ears and chanted: "La La La."

Duke rolled his eyes at me. "Okay, I get it, need to know basis only."

I said I would meet with Marian Wolinsky and Adam's therapist. We were just about finished when company arrived. A pretty redhead in a skin-tight dress and stiletto heels marched over to us looking furious. She glared at Duke and then slapped him hard across the face. I don't know why I was surprised.

"You pig! I can't believe you're cheating on me with *her!*"

"But Darlin', it's not how it looks, this is business!" Duke jumped up and continued his patter of explanations, trying to catch a break.

I had to cover my mouth to keep from laughing. This was how I'd met Duke. His life seemed to be one long parade of angry women. I wondered if this one could afford a billboard...

CHAPTER 14

When I spoke with Dr. Simon the next morning, he agreed we had a lot to discuss and suggested meeting at his Plantation office at noon. Plantation is west of Hollywood and a twenty minute drive, so I left at 11:30, to account for traffic. My GPS showed that his office wasn't far from Plantation General Hospital. It's not a coincidence that lawyers have offices near the courthouse and doctors have theirs near the hospital; everyone wants easy access in case of emergency. Different kinds of emergencies, though...

In addition to Susan Doyle's polygraph question, I wanted to ask Dr. Simon if there was a safe way to question Adam. I needed to know why he said he was sorry when he saw Spike's body; what 'bad thing' he did, why he thought it was his fault. Adam could be the key to finding the killer, if only he could communicate what he knew.

Dr. Simon's waiting room reminded me of a yoga studio: warm colors, new age music with nature sounds woven in, and a basket of herbal teas by the water cooler. There were no magazines on the table, only self-help books about finding happiness and inner peace, and some funny books of comic strips. Dr. Simon (or his decorator) had mastered the concept of Feng Shui. I really felt harmonized with my environment. And for people on the autism spectrum, like Adam, who can't tolerate jarring external stimuli, this room was perfect.

Maybe it was the soothing cocoon of the waiting room, but as soon as I met Dr. Simon, I felt like I could trust him. A trim man in his fifties, he had an engaging smile and an openness that was welcoming. With his receding salt and pepper hair and wire-rimmed glasses, he reminded me of my old evidence professor, the one who gave me my only 'C in law school. I'd try not to hold that against him.

"Hello, Jamie, thanks for coming in," he said, shaking my hand. "Let's go to my office so we can talk."

I won't bore you by describing the office; suffice it to say, it was more of the same. And the chairs were super comfortable. I wondered if his decorator could make my house look like that...

"Jamie," Dr. Simon said, his intense gaze never wavering from my face, "I'm very concerned about Adam, I believe he's in crisis. Specifically, he is experiencing cognitive dissonance brought on by post-traumatic stress disorder, or PTSD, for short."

"Isn't PTSD what war vets have?" I squirmed in my chair. I wasn't expecting this.

"Yes, but it can affect anyone who has suffered a traumatic event, and Adam was severely traumatized by his teacher's murder. Adam is particularly vulnerable because of his Asperger's. He just doesn't have the coping skills." Dr. Simon took off his glasses and tiredly rubbed his eyes.

"What's cognitive dissonance? Is that part of PTSD?" I was trying to wrap my head around all of this.

"Cognitive dissonance is a feeling of discomfort resulting from holding two conflicting beliefs simultaneously. In Adam's case, he believes he somehow caused Spike's death, but he also believes he would never do anything to hurt people he cares about. He cannot reconcile these beliefs."

There was a tightness in my chest that wouldn't let up. It was like an iron claw squeezing the air out of my lungs.

"Isn't there anything you can do for him?" I asked.

"There are things we can try, but everyone reacts differently. One way to treat PTSD is to help the patient "reframe" the trauma situation to understand it in a new way. Adam's been having nightmares and so we've been working on dream revision therapy. That's a tool for reducing cognitive conflict which doesn't address the trauma itself. Sometimes it's enough to just treat the symptoms."

"Is it working?" I was pretty sure I knew the answer already.

Dr. Simon shook his head.

"What about medications?"

Dr. Simon referred to the chart on his desk. "Adam doesn't do well with medications. In the past, we've tried several anti-anxiety medications, as well as a few different anti-depressants. None of them helped, and some have made him worse." His shoulders slumped in defeat.

I couldn't accept that we were out of options. "Surely, there's something else you can try?"

"Hypnotherapy can be effective in treating PTSD--but there *is* a risk. Reliving a traumatic event, even under hypnosis, can cause further trauma. In other words, he could get worse. Adam is so fragile right now, I'm afraid he might become suicidal. Nevertheless, I believe it's his best option at this point, and his mother agrees. We're planning to start tomorrow."

My arms were crossed tightly across my chest and I was rocking back and forth slightly in my chair. I realized I was comforting myself the way Adam does. Maybe, deep in our DNA, we are all wired to respond that way.

I looked up at Dr. Simon. "I came here to ask you if Adam would be able to take a polygraph."

Dr. Simon looked horrified. "Are you saying he's a suspect in the murder?" I could feel my eyes tearing up. I nodded.

He jumped out of his chair, shaking with anger. "That would destroy him. I won't allow it!"

CHAPTER 15

It was a relief to know Dr. Simon was fighting for Adam, too, and I said so. Then, I told the doctor about my search for evidence to eliminate Adam as a suspect and how I believed that Adam, himself, held the answers. If only we could discover why he felt so guilty...

"Exposing the roots of the trauma is one of the goals of hypnotherapy," Dr. Simon said. "You and I have the same goal, but for different reasons." He smiled and it made me feel like all was not lost.

"Would I be able to watch your hypnotherapy session with Adam tomorrow?"

He shook his head. "I'm afraid not. Although his mother authorized me to speak freely with you, your presence would distract Adam. The observer would influence the observation in this case."

Then it came to me! I may not Tweet, but I wasn't a total Luddite when it came to technology. "Could I watch it over Skype?"

Dr. Simon laughed. "Of course! I'm sorry I didn't think of it, myself."

After we discussed the details, I asked him the question that had been gnawing at me. "Is there anything you can do to protect Adam if they press charges next week?"

He answered so quickly, he'd clearly thought about it already. "If intense hypnotherapy doesn't work, I'm recommending residential treatment for Adam. The best facility for him is located in New York and he'll need to stay for at least 30 days."

I grinned. I'd been right to trust Dr. Simon.

~

I was driving home when my cell rang. It was Duke.

"Miss me yet, Darlin'?"

"I don't know how I lived without you all this time." I said, laughing. "Did you patch things up with your girlfriend?"

"Let's just say, she was very happy with me before the night was over."

"WTMI, Duke! Hearing about your sex life

wasn't part of the deal--" I almost blew through a red light, I was so busy yelling at Duke.

"Fine fine, don't get your panties in a twist. I have news for you."

"That's great! Whatcha got?"

"Well, I checked into your boy, Spike. Turns out his real name was Melvin Duane Shiprock. What kinda name is Melvin?" Duke was snickering.

"This, from the guy whose name is *Marmaduke?*"

"Marmaduke Broussard was my granddaddy's name and he was the best damn sports fisherman in Shreveport, Louisiana, I'll have you know."

"So, you're Marmaduke Broussard, the Second?"

"Third, actually."

"Well, I'm sure your granddaddy would be proud of how you're carrying on the family legacy," I said, trying not to laugh.

"You speak the truth, young lady. Now, back to Melvin, I talked to the guy who owns the diner next door and he told me our guy ate breakfast there the morning he died."

"And that's interesting...why?"

"He didn't eat alone. He was with another dude and they had a huge argument."

"Wow! But how do we find out who it was?"

"Way ahead of you, Darlin'. I showed diner guy pictures of Steve Michaels--that's the music teacher with the restraining order--and also the Zombie guys. And he ID'd one of 'em."

"You're killing me, Duke! Who was it?" I had just pulled into my driveway, but I stayed in the car.

"Darryl, the guitarist for The Zombies."

"Great job, Duke! You're amazing!" This was turning out to be a good day.

"There's more, Darlin'. Spike's credit card shows he charged a hotel room the night before he died, so I went there and talked to the front desk clerk. Turns out Spike had a lady friend with him."

Terrific...

"I showed the clerk the one picture I had, and guess what?"

"I'm afraid to ask..." I said.

"It was Rosa Michaels, Steve Michaels' better half."

"So, now we have two suspects? Daryl and Steve?"

"Yup. And, according to Spike's cell phone records, he talked to both of them the night before he died."

Chapter 16

"So, what do we do next?" I was so excited, I couldn't think straight.

"Well, I don't know about you, but I'm on my way to talk to Rosa Michaels," Duke said.

"Okay, I'll call Marian Wolinsky and try to set up a meeting with her. Let me know what you find out from Rosa. And Duke?"

"Yeah, Darlin'?"

"Try not to hit on her. I hear she has a jealous husband!" I laughed and hung up before he could say anything.

It was way past lunch time and I was starving, so the first thing I did when I got in the house was make a sandwich--a peanut butter, banana, and honey sandwich, to be exact. Now, I know what you're thinking, you're thinking that sounds gross, but you shouldn't knock it 'til you've tried it. I mean, it's not like I suggested you eat a sardine sandwich. Yes, somebody actually eats those. If you Google sardine sandwich, recipes pop up, I kid you not.

After a delightful dessert of dark chocolate (it's good for me, right? I heard that somewhere), I hunted up Marian Wolinsky's phone number, which I'd copied from Spike's probate file at the courthouse. I thought about calling Grace, but decided to wait until I heard from Duke. I was dying to hear what Rosa Michaels would say to him.

So--you know how you imagine what a person looks like after hearing their voice on the phone? Well, the opposite is true, too. Once you've seen a photograph of someone, you think you know what they sound like. I'm only telling you this because when I called Marian Wolinsky, the biker chick with multiple tattoos, I was blown away. She sounded like an educated New Yorker, with an attitude to match. I thought for sure I had the wrong Marian Wolinsky, but no, it was her. When I told her I was Adam Muller's lawyer, she said, "I have nothing more to say, I already talked to the cops." Before she could hang up, I told her I was also Adam's cousin, and that we were worried he was suicidal, and how much I'd appreciate a few minutes of her time. She softened her tone then and agreed to speak with me, for Adam's sake. We decided to meet at the Starbucks on Young Circle at four-thirty.

I arrived early and waited for Marian to rumble in on a Harley, but she drove up in a new VW, her tattoos discreetly hidden by long sleeves. She was wearing a lot of make-up and her hair was swept back into a high ponytail. She looked like the sophisticated sister of the girl on the website. I wasn't sure which one was the real Marian.

I introduced myself and we ordered coffee. She took hers black, no frou-frou Frappuccino for her.

"How's Adam doing?" she asked. "He's a good kid. Everyone at the Screaming Zombie liked him." She was tapping her long nails on the table, antsy, like she couldn't wait to get this over with.

"Adam's not doing well, I'm sorry to say. Finding Spike's body was quite a shock for him. He's having nightmares and he's not eating..."

She looked sympathetic. "Well, it's no wonder. Adam and Spike were such good buddies. Between the music and the dogs, those two had a lot in common. Adam even got along with Beast, who is not the friendliest dog, believe me." She pronounced 'dog' as 'dawg'.

"Marian, I promise to make this fast, but can you answer a few questions for me?"

"I'll try," she answered without much enthusiasm.

I pulled out Susan Doyle's list of questions. "Did Spike have any enemies?"

She laughed hollowly. "Sure, he had a lot of enemies--he was kind of an asshole--but nobody who would've killed him."

"Did he owe anyone money or did anyone owe him any money?"

"Nobody owed him any money, but the Screaming Zombies thought he owed them money. They didn't like that he used the name of the band for his store. They were suing him, but they couldn't have killed him."

"Why not?" I asked, wondering how she could be so sure.

"Because they didn't have the guts! I know those guys for a long time; me and Spike go way back, and I'm telling you they are too chickenshit for that."

"Could it have been a robbery gone wrong?" I asked, sticking to Susan's script.

"Nah. There was nothin' missing. I'm the bookkeeper, so I would know." She finished off her coffee.

I knew she was ready to bolt, so I gave up on the questions and asked her point-blank, "Who do you think killed Spike? Best guess."

"I'll tell you who did it--I think it was Steve

Michaels. He and Rosa were always fighting like crazy, yelling and screaming, and she just filed for divorce. He was super jealous."

"What's that got to do with Spike?"

"He was sleepin' with her."

CHAPTER 17

"How long had Spike and Rosa been sleeping together?" I asked.

A look of disgust crossed her face so quickly, I almost missed it. "Who knows? Who cares?" she said, flippantly.

It looked to me like maybe she cared. "Did Spike have any other girlfriends, or ex-girlfriends?"

"He was a rock star, what do you think? There were always groupies and skanks hanging around him."

She put her purse on her shoulder and pushed her chair back to stand up. I felt like I did when I was in court and the judge said, "Wrap it up, counselor, we're out of time."

"What about you?" I asked.

She narrowed her eyes. "What *about* me?"

"Well, were you and Spike ever together, as a couple?"

She shook her head and her ponytail swung back and forth. "We used to hook up, but that was a long time ago. Ancient history. Anyway, I gotta go. Good luck with Adam, give him my best." And she was gone.

I finished my coffee and soaked up some sun, while I thought about our conversation. Marian seemed convinced that Steve was the murderer, but how reliable was she? Did she have her own ax to grind? My reverie was interrupted by a beep announcing I had a text. I looked at my phone and read, "For a good time, call Duke." Then a second text, "Satisfaction guaranteed!" I figured I'd better call him before his texting turned into sexting.

"What took you so long, Darlin'?"

"Hey Duke! Sorry, I know thirty seconds is a long time to wait. What'd you find out?"

"You go first."

I propped my feet up on the chair across from me and got comfortable. "Marian Wolinsky is a riddle, wrapped in a mystery, inside a New Yorker. Not sure if she has her own agenda, but she says Steve Michaels is the guy, that he was jealous because Spike and Rosa were sleeping together."

Duke gave a low whistle of surprise. "That just confirms the PI's motto--'Everybody lies'."

I sat up in my chair. "That's the lawyer's motto, too, and they don't teach it in law school. Who's lying?"

"I think it's your girl, 'cause I believe mine. Rosa says she and Spike never did the dirty deed. He took her to a hotel to get her away from Steve, who was acting all crazy and threatening to kill her. She was scared, and people don't lie about being scared."

"Does she think Steve killed Spike?"

"That's the funny part, she doesn't think so. She said he never threatened anyone else. He was jealous as hell, but he always took it out on her."

"But why would Marian lie? Maybe she really believed they were sleeping together. I mean, if she saw them go to a hotel, of course she'd think that. So, what should we do next?"

"You leave it to me, Darlin'. I'll figure out where Steve was at the time of the murder. And I'm not ruling out the Zombie guy, Daryl, I'll check him out, too."

"Thanks, Duke! I still think Adam knows something. I'm going to watch his hypnotherapy session tomorrow morning. Why don't we touch base after that?"

"Darlin', you can touch anything you want. I wouldn't mind a bit."

CHAPTER 18

I'd just gotten home and was about to feed the cat that didn't even pretend to like me when Grace called.

"Wow! You must be psychic. I was about to call you..." I said

"Jamie," Grace said, "You're not going to believe this. I just spoke with Susan Doyle--she said Rosa Michaels was run over and killed this afternoon! Witnesses say the driver was gunning for her. Her husband Steve's been arrested and they want to pin Spike's murder on him, too. Their theory is love triangle gone bad. So, Adam's off the hook for now, maybe for good."

"I don't even know what to say..." I sat down in my armchair, trying to absorb this bombshell.

"Aren't you happy? This is great news."

"Not for Rosa Michaels," I pointed out.

"I know, I know. The poor girl...she married a killer. It happens way too often. Are you going to call your aunt and tell her the news?"

My head was spinning. "Yeah, I will. She'll be relieved. She didn't know Adam was about to be charged, but I'm sure she was worried about it. Her main concern is still Adam--he's a mess."

"Maybe if he knows they arrested Steve, he'll feel better?" Grace suggested.

"I don't know; I'll leave that up to Dr. Simon. I've already tried playing detective; I'm not ready to dabble in psychotherapy!"

"How about retail therapy?" Grace laughed.

"That, I can handle." I said. We made a date to get together for shopping and dinner the following weekend and hung up.

I felt conflicted. I was relieved Adam wasn't going to be arrested, but it still felt like a piece of the puzzle was missing. I decided not to tell Duke right away--let him finish checking out Steve's whereabouts for the time of the murder. And Adam was still suffering. I wasn't sure that Steve's arrest would make a difference to him. I knew I'd be counting the hours until his hypnotherapy the next morning. I settled in for a long night.

CHAPTER 19

It took two espressos to pry my eyes open in the morning. Although I must've gotten *some* sleep in between watching re-runs of "Friends" and "30 Rock," it sure didn't feel like it. I was nervous, but I wasn't sure why. I could've used some comic relief right about then. Where's Duke when you need him?

At 10:00, I called Dr. Simon over Skype and we confirmed that we could see and hear each other. Then he temporarily draped a towel over the screen, so Adam wouldn't see me when he came in. He removed it after Adam was lying comfortably on the sofa.

Contrary to popular belief, no shiny object is

required for hypnosis. It was simply a deep relaxation exercise with Dr. Simon making suggestions in a voice as soft as cotton. Adam looked like he was asleep, but he was still able to respond to questions. First, Dr. Simon asked him to rate his anxiety on a scale of 1-5 with a specific description for each number. Then, he told Adam to picture himself riding an elevator in a building with five floors and he was the only one who could push the buttons. If he started feeling anxious, all he had to do was ride the elevator to a lower floor.

"Do you like elevators, Adam?" Dr. Simon asked.

"Yes..."

"Don't forget to push the buttons when you need to, Adam. You are in a safe place. Nothing can hurt you here. Do you feel safe now?"

"I feel safe."

Then Dr. Simon asked him some neutral questions about his dogs before asking the next question.

"Do you know a dog named Beast?"

"Spike's dog. Like drummer...Led Zeppelin."

"Do you like Beast?"

"Beast is a good dog. He likes to play."

"When is the last time you saw Beast, Adam?"

Adam started flailing. "I hear him barking...he's upset. Why is he barking? Where is Spike? I can't go in there! No no!"

Dr. Simon backed off. "It's okay, Adam. You don't have to go in there. Don't forget about your elevator buttons. Take a deep breath and let it go. Push the number one button and ride the elevator down. Do you feel better?"

"Yes..."

"Now, Adam, you don't have to go in the room where Beast is, but I need to ask you about that day, okay?"

No answer.

"Adam, you said you did a bad thing. What was the bad thing?"

Tears started rolling down Adam's face.

"Adam, listen to me. I know you think you did a bad thing, but you didn't. Maybe you made a mistake, but you did not do anything wrong. Okay?"

No answer.

"Adam, please repeat after me. I didn't do anything wrong."

Adam started shaking his head from side to side.

"Adam, listen to me." Dr. Simon said gently. "You didn't do anything wrong. I am sure of it. Now, can you repeat after me?"

"Okay."

"Can you say this for me? I didn't do anything wrong."

In a voice so low I almost couldn't hear him, Adam said "I didn't do anything wrong."

"Good! Now what was the bad thing?"

"I didn't mean to do it! I'm sorry, Spike. It's my fault, all my fault!"

"Adam, listen to me. Let's pretend you're a fly. Can you do that?"

"Yes."

"Can you feel your pretend wings?"

"Uh huh."

"Okay, now you're a fly and you're watching Adam do the thing he thinks is bad. Tell me about it. You're a fly that can speak...just pretend."

"Adam is playing music with Spike. They're laughing. Adam asks "What's your favorite song Spike? Spike is smiling. He says 'Rosalinda's Eyes'... it reminds him of Rosa..."

"Who is Rosa?" Dr. Simon asks.

"She's a teacher. She's pretty."

"Then what happened? Remember, you're still pretending you're a fly."

"Adam asks Spike if he loves Rosa. Spike says yes. But it's a secret...don't tell."

"Then what happened?"

"Adam broke his promise! Why did you do that, Adam? You're bad!"

"How did Adam break his promise?" Dr. Simon prodded.

"He told! He promised, but he told anyway..."

"Who did Adam tell?"

No answer.

"I'm talking to our pretend fly now, Mr. Fly, who did Adam tell?

"So angry! Broken pictures, sharp! My finger hurts...I'm sorry I'm sorry I'm sorry!"

"Who is angry?"

"I can't tell you."

"Adam, did you tell Steve the secret?"

"No."

"Who did you tell?"

Adam started pulling his hair. "She was so mad!"

"Take a deep breath. Push the button and ride the elevator down. Can you do that?"

"Yes."

"Do you feel better, Adam?" Dr. Simon was speaking softly.

"Better..."

"Let's play a guessing game, okay? Was it Rosa, did you tell Rosa?"

"No...Rosa is nice."

"It's okay if the fly tells me who was mad."

Adam started shaking and crying. "Spike is dead! Spike was my best friend..."

"Adam, did you hurt Spike?"

"NO!"

"Then it's not your fault. Do you hear me? It is not your fault. Repeat after me: it is not my fault."
"It's...it's....not...m-m-my fault..."
"Now tell me, Adam, who was mad?"
"It was...Marian!"

CHAPTER 20

Marian must've killed Spike! Just yesterday, I'd been chatting with her and drinking coffee. I felt a chill go down my spine. Now, what do I do?

I watched Dr. Simon coax Adam out of his hypnotic state. I was worried that Adam would be feeling worse after all he'd been through, but, to my surprise, he looked better. Not carefree, more like a weight had been lifted off of him. He even gave Dr. Simon a half-smile. Although he was much taller now, Adam still looked like that sleepy little boy I used to babysit, reading animal stories under the covers before he drifted off.

You'd think I'd know what to do next, considering all of the mysteries I've read and all the TV shows I've watched, but I was clueless. I knew one thing for sure, I had to tell Grace! I hated doing it by text, but she was at work and I couldn't wait. Patience is not my forte.

Hey G, things just got interesting! Adam had a breakthrough under hypnosis & told us the "bad" thing he did, the one that got Spike killed...

OMG!! Why would you leave me hanging like that? Why so mean?

LOL!! He revealed a secret that Spike asked him not to tell, the secret was...

I'm going to kill you!!!!

The secret was that Spike was in love with Rosa! Adam spilled the beans and told someone who got very, very angry....

You will pay for this torture. I promise you.

Drum roll please....it was Marian!!!

No- way!!!

Yes! And now I can add "coffee klatch with a murderer" to my resume. Maybe I can get a job with the prison system...

Wow! But how do you know for sure it was her?

I don't, but my gut tells me it's her. And Adam believes it.

You have to go to the state attorney with this.

But I hate that guy! Don't make me talk to him!

Jamie....

Sigh. Okay, but you just ruined my day.

Now we're even. Lol! Good luck!

It only took me a minute to realize I couldn't go to Nick the state attorney and accuse Marian of killing Spike in a jealous rage--not because he was my arch-enemy, playing Magneto to my Professor Xavier--but because he'd never believe me. I mean, what proof did I have? Because my hypnotized, traumatized, autistic cousin said so? That would go over well. What I needed was proof. I needed Duke, damn it!

Where was he, anyway? It was weird that I hadn't heard from him, not even a lewd text. I called him, but it went to voice mail. I texted him and got no response. I made myself a piece of toast and then called the only place I could think of.

"It's always Mardi Gras at The Big Easy, this is Brendan, how may I help you?"

"Hi Brendan, I'm looking for Duke Broussard, have you seen him?"

"Um, well...Duke?" I could hear Duke in the background saying "I'm not here."

"Brendan?"

"Yes ma'am. I'm sorry but--"

"Brendan, this is Mr. Broussard's attorney and I must speak with him immediately. Please put him on the phone."

"Yes ma'am, okay--alright, here he is."

I heard the phone changing hands and then Duke said hello, but he didn't sound right, not at all.

"Duke? What's the matter? Are you sick, do you need me to take you to the hospital?"

"Don't need no hospital." He was slurring, like he'd been drinking heavily. Something was way off. Alcohol makes some people depressed, but not Duke. He was usually the happiest drunk on the planet.

"You stay there, Duke! I'll see you in five minutes." I threw on some jeans and a t-shirt, jumped in my car and raced over to The Big Easy. I used to lead such a quiet life, what the hell happened? It seemed like there was a new crisis every day. Maybe I should get a siren for the roof of my car, and paint the door panel to say: "Hang on, I'm on my way!"

Oh, Duke! You were supposed to save me, not the other way around...

CHAPTER 21

When I got to The Big Easy, I saw a swarm of barflies flitting around the outside bar, mostly tourists, but no Duke. I marched inside, on a mission to rescue Duke from his demons, himself, or whatever. It was dark in there after the glare outside and I had to wait for my eyes to adjust. Then I saw him, hunched over the bar, where it looked like he'd been all night. Unshaven, he was wearing rumpled clothes and an air of despair

I touched him lightly on the shoulder. "Duke, you okay? Did something happen?"

He shook his head, too miserable to talk.

I sat down next to him. "Is there something I can do for you?" Not one lascivious suggestion came out of his mouth--and I'd given him the perfect set-up.

Something was seriously wrong. I just sat with him for a while, neither of us saying anything. Brendan, the bartender, brought me a glass of water. After about fifteen minutes, Duke looked at me with tears in his eyes.

"I could've saved her, Jamie. That sweet girl told me she was scared, she said he'd try to kill her...but I said, 'Don't worry, you'll be okay.' And now she's dead, Rosa's dead! That jealous bastard killed her. Just like he killed Spike." Duke laid his head on the bar in defeat.

"Duke! It's not your fault," I said, patting him gently on the back. "And Steve didn't kill Spike."

Duke looked at me like I was crazy. "What the hell are you saying, Jamie?"

"It was Marian. She had a little jealousy problem herself."

"Damn, Jamie! These people are nuts!"

"That's saying a lot, coming from you, Duke!" I laughed, and then he did, too.

"Why are you here, anyway?" he asked, perking up a little.

"I came here to save you. Well, most of you. Your liver is a lost cause, I'm afraid."

Even Brendan the bartender smiled at that.

"Actually," I said, "I came to tell you that Adam's in the clear, but I still need your help. If we're going to take Marian down, I need proof I can take to the state attorney, that smug little weasel. You in?"

"You bet I am, Darlin'. But what do you say to some breakfast first? What are you havin', a Bloody Mary or a Mimosa?"

CHAPTER 22

After a breakfast of scrambled eggs with a side of grits (minus the Mimosa), I helped Duke find a taxi to take him home; he was in no condition to drive. Then I headed over to Aunt Peg's house; I wanted to check on Adam after his rough morning and bring my aunt up to speed.

My aunt opened the door before I could knock and ushered me in. She gave me a quick hug and whispered, "Hey Jamie."

I whispered back, "Why are we whispering?"

She pointed at the sofa where Adam was sleeping with Angus, the Scottish terrier, dozing on his chest, and Bono, the Irish setter, crashed out on the floor. I followed her into the kitchen where we could sit and chat.

"How's he doing after this morning?" I asked.

She smiled. "Dr. Simon was so pleased with the progress they made. He thinks that, given time, Adam will be back to his old self. In fact, as we were driving home, Adam said, "Mom, I miss Spike."

"I'm so happy to hear that! And I have more good news for you--the state attorney doesn't believe Adam had anything to do with Spike's murder. He thinks it was Steve Michaels, the music teacher." I decided not to throw Marian into the mix.

"Oh, thank God! But, poor Rosa...I heard on the news she'd been killed, do they think that was Steve, too?"

"They do."

She shook her head sadly. "Jamie, she was the nicest woman, so kind and caring--what a tragedy!"

"It won't bring her back, but I'm confident justice will prevail."

"I hope so," my aunt said.

As we were saying our good-byes, I thought of something. "The last time I was here, I forgot to look at Adam's "music stuff" in his room. I feel bad, what did he want to show me?"

Aunt Peg thought for a second. "Oh, I know what it was! He wanted to show you the video recordings of him playing different instruments."

"Oh, he records himself?"

"No, Spike recorded all of their lessons."

Chapter 23

"Really? Tell me more about that," I said.

"I'm not sure, but I think Spike installed a camera in the ceiling to record all the lessons."

"Good to know."

We said our good-byes after I'd promised to come for dinner on Sunday. My dance card was full these days!

What I had to do next was so unpleasant I almost talked myself out of it. *Just get it over with, Jamie, like ripping off a Band-Aid.* So I did it. I went home and called him, the snarky state attorney, my sworn enemy, Nick Dimitropoulos. He didn't even say "Hello." Such a pleasant fellow.

"If you called to read me any more statutes,

Quinn," he said, "don't bother. We have a new suspect."

As soon as I heard his voice, I pictured him, from his slicked-back hair all the way down to his shiny shoes. I felt my blood pressure rising.

"Well, Nick, you know how you had the wrong guy last time? You're two for two. Steve Michaels didn't do it."

"First of all, I didn't say your client's been cleared as a suspect, and, second, why do you care if we have the wrong guy? Or is he your cousin, too?" I could almost see him sneer through the phone.

"So what if Adam's my cousin? It's not like I lied about it. And I care because the real murderer's still out there. Isn't it your job to protect the public?"

"You're thinking of the police, but I get your point. Who is it, then?" He sounded genuinely curious.

"It's not a guy at all. It's a woman--Marian Wolinsky. She was Spike's bookkeeper and bitter ex-girlfriend."

"Interesting theory, Quinn, but where's your proof? I'm sure her prints and DNA are all over the crime scene, maybe because she worked there."

"Are you always this sarcastic, or am I special? The proof is in the camera Spike hid in the ceiling. You may have the murder on film."

Take that, you smug son-of-a-bitch, I thought.

"I'll check it out, Quinn...and, um, thanks for the tip."

"You're welcome." That was a surprise. Maybe there was hope for him. Anything's possible.

After I hung up, I wondered--what if the camera hadn't been recording? Then what?

CHAPTER 24

I CLEARLY NEEDED A BACK-UP PLAN, SO I SAT down at my computer and opened up the website for Florida department of motor vehicles. I knew that Marian drove a silver Volkswagen Jetta because I'd seen it at Starbucks, but I wanted to know what Steve Michaels drove. It turned out to be a Toyota Corolla, also silver. I pulled up the news story of Rosa's murder and learned that it was a small silver car that had run her over. None of the witnesses could identify the make of the car, or whether the driver was a man or a woman. Looking at them side by side, I saw the Corolla was very similar to the Jetta. Of course it was! Because nothing's ever easy. But then I had to ask myself, if Adam was now in the clear, why didn't I just walk away?

If I walked away, I could go back to my life and never have to deal with Slick Nick again, or chase around town looking for Duke. But I knew the answer. I couldn't go back to my old life because I had no life. I'd been living in the shadows, doing nothing, seeing no one, just existing. All I did was rattle around an empty house all day, keeping company with a cat that hissed at me. And, if you didn't count the stress, panic, fear and aggravation I'd been through in the past few weeks, this was the most fun I'd had in years. And it was a challenge I could sink my teeth into. When this was over, I needed to get back into the world. Why hadn't I seen it before?

As I contemplated my life, I walked over to the freezer in search of something to microwave. It was dinnertime and I was starving. While I waited for my vegetarian burrito to cook, I fed my ungrateful cat. Then I heard a beep and thought my burrito was done, but it was Duke calling on my cell.

"Hey, Darlin', I got just one question."

"What's that?"

"Where the hell's my car?"

CHAPTER 25

"You really don't remember?" I asked.

"Well, sort of, some of it. Not really..." Duke sounded embarrassed.

"Jeez, Duke. Maybe it's time for a twelve step program. You went home in a taxi because you were drunk, so--where is your car?"

"The Big Easy?"

"Yup." I took my burrito out of the oven and covered it in salsa.

"Can you give me a ride over there in the mornin'?"

"Sure thing," I said, and then I caught him up on everything he'd missed: Adam's revelation under hypnosis, Spike's camera in the ceiling, my conversation with Nick D., and the two silver cars that looked alike.

Duke whistled under his teeth. "This story just keeps gettin' weirder. When you pick me up tomorrow, let's stop at that hotel Rosa stayed at. I have an idea."

"Are you being serious, or is this one of your less raunchy pick-up lines?"

"Ouch, that hurts! Of course I'm being serious. You'd know if it was a pick-up line. Nobody ever accused *me* of being subtle."

I laughed. "If they did, they'd be lying."

∼

Duke lived in a fourplex on Roosevelt Street. It looked nice enough, the yard was kept up, and there was a kid's bike in front of the farthest door. He looked none the worse for wear when he slid into the passenger seat. He was clean-shaven and he smelled good.

"Hey there, you doin' alright today?" he said.
"Couldn't be better, you?"
"I'm ready to kick some ass," he said.
"So, just a regular day, then?" I smiled.
He laughed. "That's right, Darlin'."
"Where to?"
Duke directed me to a small hotel called Villa

Alfredo on A1A, near the beach. He asked me to wait in the car while he went in. I turned on the radio and listened to the news on NPR. He was gone quite a while, but when he came back, he was grinning.

"Spill it," I said.

"I've got it! Witnesses say Steve Michaels was here the morning Spike got killed. He didn't do it."

"What was he doing here?" I asked. "And why would they remember him?"

"'Cause he was creeping them out! He sat in his car in front of the hotel all morning. He must've been stalking Rosa."

"That's great news! Look out Marian; we're closing in on you. Duke, you're the best!"

Duke just smiled and nodded his head. "That's what all the girls say, Darlin'."

CHAPTER 26

"Duke, let's stop at the state attorney's office. I want to tell him about this. Also, I'm dying to hear if they found Spike's video camera."

"Sure, whatever."

It was impossible to get past Nick's secretary. She insisted that we needed an appointment and she wouldn't budge. I said 'no problem' and we walked away. But once we were in the hallway, I called Nick on his direct extension and said I had information for him. When he agreed to see me, I asked him to let his secretary know. It was déjà vu walking back to her desk again, except that this time she was scowling at us. Without a word, she ushered us in, then closed the door in a huff.

"You sure know how to make friends, Quinn, I'll say that for you. What's up?" Nick asked.

"Nick, this is Duke Broussard, he's a PI who's been helping me. Duke, please tell Nick what you found out this morning."

After Duke finished, Nick looked impressed.

"That's good work, but we still have a problem proving Marian did it. We can place her at the scene, but she told police she had arrived after the murder."

"What about the camera, did you find it?" I asked, literally on the edge of my seat.

Nick frowned. "Yes and no. The camera was there and it *was* recording, but it didn't capture the murder. They must've been out of range."

The three of us sat there, absorbing that information. And then something clicked in my brain.

"That's still good news," I said.

"What the heck, Jamie?" Duke muttered.

"How do you figure?" asked Nick.

"Marian doesn't know about the camera! If she did, she would've erased it or taken it down," I said.

"So what? Duke said.

I just smiled. "Watch and learn, boys." I took out my cell phone and called Marian. I still had her number in my phone from our Starbucks meeting. My call went straight to voicemail, like I hoped it would.

After the beep, I said: "This is Jamie Quinn, sorry to bother you, but I have a quick question. Adam told me Spike had a camera in the ceiling to record his lessons. Before I tell the police, I want to know if it's true. Could you let me know? Thanks."

I turned to Nick. "You need to send someone over to *The Screaming Zombie* because she's going over there to grab that camera."

Duke looked quizzical. "How do you know she'll listen to the message?"

"Because she's cautious," I said. "She needs to know if anyone's onto her, so, of course, she'll listen to her voicemail. Once she hears about the camera, she'll race over there to destroy it. She doesn't know there's nothing on it." I was feeling pretty smug, I must admit.

Nick leaned back in his chair and smiled. "Not bad, Quinn," he said. Then he picked up the phone on his desk and made some calls. When he was done, the trap had been set. We just had to wait for Marian to make her move.

CHAPTER 27

"She almost fell off the ladder when the police barged in!"

Grace and I were sitting in her office and I was telling her how I'd outsmarted Marian. Actually, how *we* had outsmarted Marian because, without Grace and Duke, Susan Doyle and Adam, Aunt Peg and yes, even Nick Dimitropoulos, Marian would've gotten away with murder.

"I love it! I would've paid money to see the look on her face," Grace said.

"But wait, there's more," I said.

"I'm waiting," Grace said, drumming her fingers on the desk. "And not patiently either."

"Not only was Marian taken away, so was her

car, and it turned out to be the other murder weapon." I let that sink in.

Grace gasped. "She killed Rosa, too!"

"She was crazy with jealousy. She thought Spike and Rosa were sleeping together. She probably wouldn't have cared about that, actually, since Spike slept around, but, when Adam told her Spike was in love with Rosa, Marian totally lost it."

Grace looked thoughtful. "So, there really was a love triangle, just not the one we thought. Marian loved Spike, Spike loved Rosa, and Rosa?"

"She still loved Steve, her high school sweetheart, even after he was so abusive."

"But what happened with Spike, do we know?"

"Here's the timeline: the night before the murder, Spike took Rosa to a hotel to protect her from Steve. We know that Spike received calls that night from both Steve and Daryl, one of the Zombies. Steve was probably looking for Rosa. The next morning, Spike had breakfast with Daryl at the diner next door and they had an argument. Then, after breakfast, Spike went to the music store where Marian was waiting. She was furious because she thought he'd spent the night with Rosa. She started screaming at him and then she totally lost it, picked up Adam's didgeridoo and whacked Spike on the head. When she realized what she'd done, she left the building so she could pretend she arrived later.

Poor Adam walked in a few minutes later and found Spike dead on the floor."

"Wow! That's some story," Grace said. "You can't make stuff like that up. I mean, who would've imagined a didgeridoo could be a deadly weapon?"

"No one, especially since nobody even knows what a didgeridoo is!" I laughed.

"I think this is a great excuse to go out and celebrate," Grace said.

"Since when do we need an excuse?" I asked. Just then, my phone rang. I looked at the number, and said "Sorry, I have to take this" to Grace.

"What can I do for you, Nick? Is it okay if I call you Nick? I never really asked." I laughed. "I see, okay, no problem. I'll be right there."

I looked at Grace, "Do you mind if we make a stop before we go celebrate?"

CHAPTER 28

I knocked on Aunt Peg's door. Adam answered, looking better than he had in a long time.

"Hey, Jamie!" He said, giving me a hug. "I didn't know you were coming over."

"Hi Adam! Can you help me unload my car?"

"Sure, is it something heavy?"

"See for yourself." I said, as Grace opened the car door and Beast, Spike's German shepherd, jumped out of the backseat.

"Beast!!" Adam yelled, running over to hug the dog, which gave him a big sloppy kiss. Within thirty seconds, they were playing together and rolling around on the ground.

My aunt came out of the house. "Are you sure you don't mind?" I asked her.

"It'll be fine," she said. "Look how happy you made him!"

"I think they both look pretty happy."

Grace waved from the car and my aunt waved back.

"I have to get going," I said. "We're having a 'Girls' Night Out'."

"I'd say you earned it. Thanks for everything and don't forget about dinner on Sunday.

I was about to get in the car when Aunt Peg stopped me. "Jamie, I just want to say, your mom would've been proud of you."

"She would've been proud of you too," I said, and blew her a kiss.

CHAPTER 29

"So, what's next?" Duke asked me.

I'd taken him out for a steak dinner at The Capitol Grille as a thank-you for all his help. Since I was a vegetarian, I was eating a baked potato and a salad.

"Not sure," I said, my mouth full of potato and sour cream. "How about you?"

"Some work, some play, you know me, Darlin'. Are you thinkin' about going back to being a divorce lawyer? You were damn good at it." He shoved a big piece of rare steak in his mouth.

"Maybe, at least until something better comes along. I just know it's time I got back to work."

"Maybe you could recommend me to your

lawyer friends, especially those hot lady lawyers." He smirked at me.

I shook my head and smiled. "Keep dreamin', Duke."

He pretended to look hurt.

"There is one thing I'd like to do," I said, "now that my mom is gone..."

"What's that?" Duke asked.

"I'm curious about my father. I don't know much about him, except that he was 'big trouble.' I need to know his story. I mean, maybe he's mafia, or an international art thief--or maybe he's 'the fixer' for dirty politicians. All I know is I'm going to find out."

"I'm at your service, m' lady," Duke said, tipping his imaginary hat.

"You'd help me?" I said, touched.

"What do you think, Jamie?" He was grinning. "I'd *love* to tell you who's your daddy."

I groaned and threw my napkin at him. "I don't know why I put up with you."

"Cause I'm one of a kind," Duke said with a wink.

I laughed. "That's for sure."

I realized then that I was happier than I'd been in a long time. I had a new life and people who cared about me; I even had a mystery to solve. Maybe I should design my own "Life is Good" t-shirt: one with a smiling stick figure, surrounded by friends.

Dear reader,

We hope you enjoyed reading *Death by Didgeridoo*. Please take a moment to leave a review, even if it's a short one. Your opinion is important to us.

Discover more books by Barbara Venkataraman at https://www.nextchapter.pub/authors/barbara-venkataraman

Want to know when one of our books is free or discounted? Join the newsletter at http://eepurl.com/bqqB3H

Best regards,

Barbara Venkataraman and the Next Chapter Team

You might also like:

Accidental Activist by Barbara Venkataraman

To read the first chapter for free, please head to: https://www.nextchapter.pub/books/accidental-activist

ABOUT THE AUTHOR

Award-winning author Barbara Venkataraman is an attorney in South Florida where she draws inspiration for her books from the daily headlines. She loves connecting with readers through her books and finds a particular kind of joy in a well-turned phrase. In addition to writing fiction, she co-authored *Accidental Activist: Justice for the Groveland Four* with her son Josh Venkataraman about his successful four-year quest to obtain posthumous pardons for The Groveland Four.

Lightning Source UK Ltd.
Milton Keynes UK
UKHW012158210921
390987UK00001B/102